# Twice Touched
## The Sand Beneath His Hand

Freshwater Horizon Press

Texas

*To my wife, kids, parents, brothers, extended family, and friends. I am blessed daily because of you.*

# Prologue

# The First Touch

I was no different than the rest—
a fragment of dust beneath sandals and silence.
I had known only wind, and weight,
and the restless shuffle of feet too busy to notice me.

But that morning,
the earth held its breath.
A crowd had gathered.
Their voices were thunder.
Their fingers, curled around stones.
And in the center...
He knelt.

Not to speak.

Not to argue.

But to write.


And as His finger met the earth,

it found me.


There are no words for what passed through me.

Only warmth, like the beginning of a sunrise.

Only stillness, like the sea before its birth.

Only knowing—deep, vast, eternal knowing—

that I had been seen.


He wrote. Then paused. Then wrote again.

And in that second stroke, His finger touched me
again.

Twice.

Twice, the hand that shaped galaxies pressed upon
me.


And I,

a single grain of sand,

became more than dust.

I did not follow Him.
I did not preach or bleed or rise.
But I remained.

Carried by feet that did not know me,
by winds that served unknowingly,
I have moved through centuries.
I have seen empires fall.
I have witnessed faith bloom in catacombs,
and candles lit in cathedrals.

But it always begins here—
in the hush between the crowd's shouting,
in the weight of mercy drawn into the dust,
in the moment the Word became a whisper in the
earth...

...and twice touched me.

# Chapter 1

## The Stone and the Morning

I do not remember how I arrived at the tomb.

Perhaps a robe brushed me from the temple steps.

Perhaps I clung to the hem of mourning.

Or perhaps the wind, knowing more than it lets on,

placed me precisely where I was meant to be.

I had been near death before.

Thrown near the feet of the accused.

But this place...

This was different.

The stone was sealed.

The silence, heavy.

Even the sun waited.

Then, in the breath between night and dawn,

the earth remembered something.

It trembled—not in fear,

but in awe.


The stone—

that heavy, final word—

rolled back as if it had no weight at all.


Light spilled from a place that once held shadow.

Not sunlight.

Not firelight.

But a light that remembered Eden.


And I,

resting unnoticed near the edge of that stone,

felt it first—

a warmth not of this world.


He stepped out.

Alive.

No one saw Him just then,
but I did.
Not with eyes,
but with being.

He walked past me, and the ground did not dare
whisper.
Even the wind held its breath,
as if afraid to disturb the miracle.

He was not the same as before.
The body bore wounds,
but the glory outshone them.
He had passed through death,
and it had not held Him.

And I,
the grain of sand twice touched,
felt again that echo—

That same hush as when He wrote beside me.

That same weightless mercy.

That same eternal stillness.


Women came,

bearing tears and spices.

Angels spoke,

and their wings stirred dust near my resting place.

I wished I could speak.

I wished I could tell them:


He is gone, but not lost.

He lives, and so does everything He ever
touched.


Even me.


And so I moved again,

caught in the hem of a running disciple,

carried into the world

not to preach,

not to teach,

but to remember.

To bear silent witness
to the One who walked out of the grave
as easily as He once walked on water.

# Chapter 2

## Tongues of Flame

I was carried in silence—
folded into the hem of a garment,
pressed between sandal and step,
swept upward by feet that longed for Heaven
but still clung to the dust.

The room was small,
yet wide with waiting.
Their voices were hushed,
not from fear,
but from hunger.

They did not know what they waited for—
only that He had said,
"Wait."

And so they did.
With prayers like aching stars,
with eyes that had seen too much
to ever close again.

I nestled in a corner of the floor,
unseen as always.
Yet I could feel it—
a trembling not of earth,
but of eternity leaning close.

Then, like breath from before time,
He came.

Not in sandals.
Not in flesh.
But in wind.

It filled the room,
a rushing from no direction

yet every direction.

It circled the souls gathered there

like a storm made only of fire and voice.


Then light—

not sunlight,

but flame,

descended in silence

and rested upon each of them.


Not to burn.

But to ignite.


They opened their mouths—

and out came the world's languages,

woven not in confusion,

but in understanding.


Every word like a river returning to its source.

Every sound carrying the echo of Eden's garden,

and the whisper of the One who once bent

to write in the dust.

I watched from below,
lowly as ever,
as eternity danced on their shoulders.

And I remembered His finger...
and how still the earth had gone
when He wrote mercy.

Now,
the earth stirred again—
not in silence,
but in song.

They poured into the streets
with voices not their own,
yet more truly theirs than ever before.

And I,
carried now in the fold of a zealot's robe,

heard the first sermon that needed no scroll.

He lives, they cried.
He has come.
He will not leave us alone.

I had been beneath the finger.
I had seen the stone roll away.
And now—
I had tasted fire.

And though I was only a grain of sand,
I knew this:

The dust of the earth
had become the breath of Heaven.

# Chapter 3

## From Stones to Songs

I remember the stones.

I remember the way they trembled in fists.
The way they flew, not with justice,
but with fear wrapped in fury.

And I remember the man they struck.
Stephen.
A soul who saw Heaven while standing on earth.

He did not curse.
He did not run.

He prayed.

I struck his robe as he fell.

The dust rose gently to greet him—

as if earth itself could not bear to see him lie
alone.


And then,

I settled beside a shadow.


A young man.


He did not lift a stone,

but held the coats of those who did.

His name was Saul.


I remained in his fold

as he walked away with a heart swollen by zeal

and a mind sharpened by law.


He hunted mercy

like it was a sickness to be cured.

15

Until—

the light found him.


The road to Damascus was dry and hard,

but the light that met him was neither.


It struck like thunder,

but held the gentleness of a whisper.


He fell.

Blind, but no longer blind.

Silent, but no longer deaf.


"Saul, Saul, why do you persecute Me?"


He said nothing.

But something broke.


Not like chains.

Like walls.

I was swept away again—
carried this time not by anger,
but by song.


They called him Paul now.


He bore the same eyes,
but the fire had changed.


It no longer burned to destroy.
It burned to awaken.


I lay once more in a prison,
under his feet.
Beside Silas.
Their backs bleeding,
but their lips—singing.


It was not the kind of singing men do to escape.
It was the kind angels listen for.

Then the earth remembered
what mercy sounds like.

Chains shattered.
Walls split.
Doors flew open.

But they stayed.

Not all freedom runs.

Sometimes, it waits
so that grace can catch the ones chasing it.

A jailer fell to his knees.
Paul lifted him up.

And I,
a grain of sand that once touched a martyr's blood,
now touched baptismal water.

I have seen stones rise in hate.

I have seen them fall in prayer.

I have seen the man who stood among them

become the one who set captives free.

# Chapter 4

# In the Shadow of an Empire

The sandals changed.

They were heavier now.

Not worn by fishermen or prophets,

but by soldiers whose steps claimed cities.

The stones were polished.

The air, perfumed with incense and iron.

I had entered Rome.

Here, the earth groaned under marble and myth.

Statues reached for gods

who never bent down to touch the sand.

But even in the empire of eagles,

the whisper of the Nazarene had come.


And I—

carried again by feet that never knew my
name—

was swept into its courts,

its gutters,

its shadows.


Beneath the opulence,

there were flickers of light.


In quiet rooms,

bread was broken.

Songs were sung not to Caesar,

but to Christ.


They called it ekklesia.

Not temple.

Not empire.

But gathering.

Of the poor.

Of the persecuted.

Of those who knew

there was a kingdom without borders.


I was pressed into the dust of a catacomb floor,

where lanterns flickered against walls etched with fish and crosses.


Here, faith whispered louder than fear.

They prayed not to survive,

but to stay true.


I listened.

As always.


Some spoke of Paul.

Of how he had come to Rome—not as a preacher,

but as a prisoner.

They said he had written letters from his cell,
as if paper could outlive empires.


They said his voice had not trembled.


That he knew what I already knew—
death had no hold on those who had seen
light.


One day, I felt it.
The quiet weight of sorrow.
Somewhere above,
a sword had fallen.


And the man who once stood among stones,
who sang in chains,
had met his end in silence.


But not defeat.


The city did not pause.

Empires never do.

But beneath its streets,

a trembling remained.

Not of fear,

but of foundation.


Something was cracking.

Something eternal was taking root

in the cracks of marble and the spaces
between swords.


I have seen kingdoms rise on gold and fall in
dust.

But only once

have I seen an empire tremble

because love refused to die.

# Chapter 5

## Measured and Eternal

I was chosen.

Not stepped on.

Not swept away.

But scooped—deliberately—by a calloused hand

that saw something in me I did not know how to see.

The man was a maker of glass.

He spoke little,

but his thoughts glowed like embers behind his eyes.

He poured us—

grains of sand of various shapes and hues—

into a hollowed sphere,
then sealed it with fire.

Two bulbs.
A narrow throat.
And the slow descent of time.

I fell,
again and again,
inside a world of glass.

Not by wind,
but by design.

Each fall counted.
Each second measured.
Yet I knew—
the eternal cannot be timed.

Still, they tried.

The hourglass became precious.

Not because it controlled time,

but because it made men think they could.


In ships, in courts, in monasteries,

we were turned over and over,

as prayers and arguments and letters raced
the falling of sand.


They called it clepsammia—

a thief of sand.


But I was no thief.


I was a witness.


One day,

I was shaken loose.


Not from time,

but from a crack in the glass.

Fallen, once more,

into the hem of a bishop's cloak.


And so I was carried

to a gathering of voices more thunderous
than the sea.


They called it the First Council of Nicaea.


Men from every corner of the empire,

some with eyes clouded from torture,

some with voices honed for scripture,

argued not about power,

but about truth.


Was He begotten or made?

Was He divine in essence, or only in title?

Could the infinite have walked among the
finite?


Their words clashed like swords,

but something deeper stirred the air.

I lay beneath the sandals of one who barely spoke.

He wept when others shouted.

He prayed when others postured.


And when the creed was spoken—

when the room quieted and ink touched parchment—

I felt a weight settle in the air.


Not victory.

Not certainty.


But clarity.


"Light from Light,

true God from true God..."


They spoke it together.

And for a moment,

time itself seemed to pause.

I remembered the fire of Pentecost.

The stones that rose in hate.

The chains that fell in song.

Now—

they spoke not in defense,

but in declaration.

The hourglass had shattered.

But I still remembered what it had tried to hold.

Time is not meant to contain the eternal.

Only to carry its echoes.

I have fallen in silence.

I have drifted in wind.

I have measured what could not be counted.

But only here,

in the breath between dogma and devotion,

have I seen truth poured out

30

like light through glass.

# Chapter 6

## Ink and Flame

After the voices of the council,
the world grew quiet again.

Not empty—
just reverent.

I was carried by boot and saddle,
through forests that sang in wind
and valleys where the stars felt closer than stone.

Eventually,
I settled in a place
where silence wore robes
and time passed like prayer.

A monastery.
Cold in stone,
but warm in spirit.

They called themselves scribes.
Servants not of sword,
but of scripture.

Their hands were stained with ink,
their eyes softened by candlelight.

They did not preach.
They preserved.

Each letter drawn as if it were being born.
Each word cradled like breath.

They wrote not to impress,
but to remember.

I fell onto a table near the edge of vellum,

resting beside a curl of golden pigment

as a monk whispered aloud:


"In the beginning was the Word..."


And I felt it again—

the same weight as when He wrote beside me.

The same hush as Pentecost.

The same warmth that once cracked open a tomb.


The scribe paused.

He breathed.

He prayed.


Then dipped the quill in ink

and continued to copy eternity

one fragile syllable at a time.


Around him, others worked in stillness.

Some carved.

Some sang.

One fed the fire that kept the ink from freezing.

They did not know
that empires were rising and crumbling beyond
their walls.

They only knew
that light must be passed on—
even if by candle.

The page they completed would outlive them.
Carried across seas,
hidden in caves,
rediscovered by hands centuries away.

And I—
a grain of sand once touched by the Eternal—
rested beside a capital letter shaped like a flame.

I watched as one monk smiled,
though no one saw it.
His fingers smudged the ink

as he drew the edge of a lion's mane in gold.

He wasn't copying.
He was adoring.

I have seen kingdoms built with swords.
I have seen creeds written with thunder.
But here,
among ink and breath,
I saw the Word become beautiful again.

# Chapter 7

## Fire and Flour

Not all moments arrive with thunder.

Not all light comes in flames.

Sometimes, the sacred enters

on the back of laughter,

and settles in the dust beneath a baker's heel.

I had grown used to silence.

To ink and prayer.

To candlelight and cloistered breath.

But now—

the world sang a different song.

The air smelled of yeast and sea salt.
Children shouted in the distance.
And smoke curled joyfully from a stone oven
at the edge of a crowded street.

I had arrived in Naples.

The baker was not a monk,
but he moved with reverence.
His hands, dusty with flour,
danced across dough
as if shaping the sky.

He was poor,
but rich in wonder.

He spoke to the dough
as if it might answer back.

He rolled it thin,
spread sauce made from sun-warmed tomatoes,

added cheese like snowfall,

and crowned it with fresh basil—green, bright, alive.


Then—

into the fire.


I lay near the oven's mouth,

swept there by wind or maybe whim.


The flames licked the air like tongues of Pentecost,

but this was no upper room.

No martyr's cell.

No council or creed.


Just a man feeding his city.


When he pulled the pizza from the fire,

a crowd gathered.


They cheered.

Not for doctrine.
Not for dogma.

But for something simple,
and warm,
and shared.

A boy took the first bite
and closed his eyes
like he'd just tasted heaven.

And for a moment—
just a breath—
I remembered the silence of the tomb,
the rush of wind,
the fire on shoulders.

And I wondered...

Could the divine dwell here too—

in flour,

in fire,

in the joy of the ordinary?


I have seen kingdoms fall.

I have seen saints die.

But here,

beneath the heel of a baker,

I saw joy rise from ashes

to feed the living.

# Chapter 8

## West of the Wind

The wind came with a promise.
A direction untraveled.
A hunger wrapped in hope.

I had been resting in a coastal village,
pressed into the wood of a shipwright's bench,
when the carpenter's breath sent me sailing—
right into the grain of timber
destined to become a deck.

And so, I crossed an ocean.

The ship groaned like a cathedral in storm.
Salt curled in the air.
Sailors sang not for joy,

but to push back the silence of open sea.

They watched stars,
spoke prayers,
and feared the edge of the world.

Some called it glory.
Some called it madness.
All of them looked west.

I nestled between planks
as boots stomped above,
tracking their doubts across the boards
like questions never asked aloud.

The sky was a bruised canvas of clouds.
The waves told no secrets.
And time—once measured by hourglass—
was now measured in faith.

Then one morning,

a shout.

"Tierra!"

The word broke like lightning.

Feet scrambled.
Voices rose.
Hands pointed at the sliver of green
trembling on the edge of horizon.

Land.

They fell to their knees.
Some kissed the boards.
Others wept or laughed.

I was carried ashore
in the boot of one too stunned to speak.

The sand here felt warmer,

softer—untouched.

The trees danced without needing to be seen.
The birds called out like prophets.
And the people...
watched from the trees,
silent as shadows.

Not all arrivals are kind.
Not all discoveries are gifts.

The earth groaned beneath the steps of those
who saw it as something to name,
to claim,
to shape in their image.

Still, the wind blew gently.
Still, the sky watched.

And I—
a grain who had once rested beneath the finger of
mercy—

wondered if I was here

to witness wonder again...

or warning.


In time,

songs would change.

Languages would blend.

Tears would fall.


And yet—

so would seeds.


Cathedrals would rise beside volcanoes.

Scripture would be read beneath jungle canopy.

Crosses would be carved from strange new trees.


Even here,

the story would not be lost.


It would be rewritten in another tongue.

But still...

still it would be told.

I have crossed seas in silence.
I have landed where maps once feared to look.
And though wonder danced beside grief,
I saw in the soil of this New World
the echo of a promise:
that light, once spoken, cannot be undone.

# Chapter 9

## Words that Tremble

Not all thunder comes from sky.

Some is written.

Carefully.

With ink that bleeds more slowly than blood.

I had been tucked into a soldier's boot,

shaken loose during a march through a city

buzzing like a storm ready to break.

They called it Philadelphia.

The roads were rough.

The air smelled of horses, ink, and heated
    argument.

The people moved as if every step carried

meaning.

Because it did.

I slipped into the folds of a boot heel
and rolled beneath a door—
into a room filled not with warriors,
but with pens.

And voices.

So many voices.

Some spoke of tyranny.
Some of divine rights.
Some feared failure.
Others feared silence more.

And then,
from among them,
a document.

It lay on the table
like a tinderbox waiting for a match.

I had seen letters before.
Holy ones.
Copied with reverence under candlelight.

But this—
this was something different.

Not scripture.
But still sacred.

A cry from the dust of men
who wanted to breathe as free as the stars above
    them.

"We hold these truths to be self-evident..."

I felt the floor shift beneath me,
as if even the earth questioned the weight

of what had just been said.

"...that all men are created equal..."

The words rang loud,
even as they passed over those not seen—
the enslaved,
the silenced,
the forgotten.

But still,
the truth had been spoken.
And once truth is loosed,
it never fully returns.

One by one,
they signed.

Their hands trembled—
not with fear,
but with understanding.

That ink could invite war.
That words could ignite history.

I nestled beneath the table,
pressed between the feet of men
who would become statues and silhouettes.

And I remembered the creed of Nicaea.
The stones of Stephen.
The prison songs of Paul.

Here, too,
a new kind of faith was being born.

Not in God alone,
but in freedom.
The idea that all people bore
some glimmer of divine light
and could not be owned.

The parchment curled at its edges.

The candles burned low.

The air smelled of wax and sweat and destiny.


I have heard voices lifted in prayer.

I have heard them lifted in rebellion.

And here,

in a room filled with trembling hands and
    thunderous silence,

I heard the sound of a nation

being born through ink.

# Chapter 10

## Beneath the Floorboards

The wind had grown heavier.
Not with rain,
but with sorrow.

Chains clanked like bells in the distance.
Cotton fields bent beneath the sun
while eyes searched for a north
they had never seen—
only believed in.

And I,
once pressed into the seal of freedom,
was now carried in the folds of bondage.

I had become lodged in the shoe

of a woman who walked with quiet fire.

Her name was Ruth.
Her hands bore the memory of labor,
but her heart sang hymns in silence.

She did not run at first.
She waited.

Waited for the moon,
the signal,
the hush that meant
now.

When she stepped into the night,
she did not flee—
she followed.

Followed a river.
A whisper.
A promise that somewhere north

there were hands that would hide her,

feet that would lead her,

and songs that would remind her

she was still someone's daughter.


I fell from her shoe

inside the floorboards of a wooden room

where children slept with their mouths covered,

and prayers were mouthed, not spoken.


They called it a "station."

But no trains came here.


Only people—

carrying names they no longer used,

and hope they dared not speak aloud.


The woman who kept the house

wore a cross beneath her apron.

She baked bread in silence.

She knew when to lift the rug,

when to pour water to hide the scent,

when to weep behind the barn.


She was not a preacher.

But she preached with every act of risk.


One night,

a man passed through.


Tall.

Scarred.

Eyes like lightning waiting to strike.


He laid down in the crawlspace,

his back pressed to the ground,

his breath shallow.


I rested by his hand.


He whispered something I had heard once
    before—

a scripture carved in flame and blood:

"Let my people go."

The stars turned above.
Dogs howled far away.
A door creaked softly.

Then—
a whisper:
"It's time."

They rose.
One by one.

And walked.

They did not carry weapons.
Only names passed in secret.
Songs coded with direction.
And the echo of a God
who walked with slaves before.

I have seen roads paved in glory.

I have seen ships claim new worlds.

But here—

beneath floorboards,

inside shadows,

guided by faith and fire—

I saw a freedom more holy

than any parchment could promise.

# Chapter 11

## A Few Words, Forever

The ground was still grieving.

Grass had returned,
but beneath it,
the earth remembered blood.

Rain had come and gone,
but the dust still whispered
of boys who became men
only long enough to fall.

I arrived with the wind—
caught in the fold of a widow's coat
as she stepped quietly

into a sea of markers
no one could fully count.

The trees stood like sentinels.
The sky hung low,
as if listening.

And then—
he stepped forward.

He was taller than most,
but looked smaller in sorrow.
His coat was plain.
His face, worn.

But something in him
stood straighter than the flag.

They called him Lincoln.

Others had spoken already.

For hours.

Great speeches.

Many words.

But he held only a scrap of paper—

not to impress,

but to remember.

I settled on the steps below him,

carried there in the cuff of a soldier's boot.

And I listened.

Not as a citizen.

Not as a spectator.

But as a witness

to the silence between each word.

"Four score and seven years ago..."

The crowd shifted.

Not from boredom.

From breath.


"...a new nation, conceived in liberty..."


And I thought of Jerusalem.

Of Rome.

Of ships and scrolls and prisons.


And now,

this—

a battlefield turned altar.


He did not shout.

He did not boast.


He spoke like one

trying to honor something too large for language.


"...that this nation, under God, shall have a new
    birth of freedom..."

63

And then,
he was done.

Not ten minutes.

A few words.

But the earth had heard them.
And it remembered.

The boots that brought me here shifted again.
People dispersed,
quietly.

But something stayed—
an echo held in the dirt.

A vow not of vengeance,
but of vision.

That perhaps what was buried here
might grow.

I have stood in cathedrals.
I have rested beneath scrolls.
I have heard fire, storm, and sermon.
But never
have I heard so few words
carry so much sky.

# Chapter 12

## Bread and Ashes

They said it started with the markets.
With numbers that danced,
then fell like birds from the sky.

But I felt it first in the dust.

In the hunger that didn't just gnaw at bellies,
but at hope.

I was caught in the wool thread of a coat
that had once been gray,
but now wore the color of ash.

The man who wore it
stood in line without looking up.

His hands were weathered—
not by war,
but by waiting.

The line moved slowly.
It wound around a city block like a prayer
no one quite believed in anymore.

Children clung to their mothers.
Hats were held, not worn—
a quiet act of respect
for dignity slipping through fingers.

He didn't speak.
No one did.

Words cost more than they used to.
Silence was cheaper.
Easier to carry.

I nestled in the seam near his shoulder,

near a thread he had stitched himself with rough
   twine.

He had patched what he could.

Everything else,

he simply endured.


Inside the kitchen,

the warmth was not just from the soup.


A woman ladled bowls without pause—

no judgment,

no pity,

only grace.


She wore a small cross around her neck,

and hummed old hymns under her breath.


"Come ye weary, heavy laden..."


The man took his bowl.

He nodded.

And for the first time that day,

his lips parted—not in words,
but in breath.

Like a thaw.

He sat by the wall.
Cradled the bowl like it was porcelain.
Shared a crust of bread with the child beside him,
who wasn't his.

No one asked.
No one needed to.

I had once rested in palaces.
I had listened beneath domes,
cathedrals,
council halls.

But here,
beside bread that cracked like dry leaves,
I saw something more eternal

than marble.

He closed his eyes,
and whispered four words.

Not to be heard—
just to be remembered.

"Give us this day..."

I have seen fire fall from heaven.
I have heard angels in song.
But here,
in a line of empty hands and quiet mercy,
I saw what it means
to live by daily bread.

# Chapter 13

## Dust Upon Dust

The silence was absolute.

Not like prayer,

not like awe—

but like space itself had been holding its breath

since the stars were born.


And then... a whisper of movement.

A shadow.

A boot.


Touching down

on dust

older than Earth.


I was there.

Pressed into the tread of an astronaut's heel,
carried in a speck of soil
caught in the fabric of a uniform
stitched by hands that still believed in wonder.

We had left the garden,
and the gospels,
and the trenches,
and the breadlines...

And now we stepped onto the moon.

The stars looked no closer.
But Earth—
Earth shone like a marble suspended in song.

Blue. Fragile. Full.

The man climbed down slowly.
Every motion choreographed
by science,

faith,
and longing.

And then—
that step.

One small step.

The boot met the moon.
And I,
a grain once touched by the hand of God,
now rested on a world
where no hand had ever reached.

They planted a flag.
Gathered dust.
Took photos.
Spoke words the world would never forget.

But what I remember most
was the stillness.

Not lifeless.
Sacred.

Before they left,
one bent to collect a final rock.

A small one.
Rough-edged.
Uneven.

It crumbled slightly as they sealed it in a
    container.

A single grain of sand—me—
lodged into a crevice along the container's edge.

Unnoticed.

Preserved.

When the lander rose,

so did I.

Carried home
in silence,
through flame and friction,
tucked inside a fragment
that would sit on museum glass,
or roll unnoticed across a lab table.

I had left the moon.
But not the journey.

I have rested in cathedrals.
I have fallen in war.
I have been caught in wind,
and cradled by the stars.

But still—
I return.

To Earth.

To the place He once touched me.

To the story still unfolding.

# Chapter 14

## White Dust, White Sox

I had traveled through wars,

through whispered prayers and burning skies.

I had tasted cathedrals,

and curled beside kings.


But I had never been to a ballpark.


It was loud.

Joyfully loud.

A cathedral of another kind,

where cheers rose like hymns

and the scent of peanuts and beer replaced
   incense.


The field was sacred in its own way—

a canvas of chalk lines and destiny.

And I was here.

Not by wind,

but by popcorn.


I had fallen into a paper bag,

then onto a denim knee,

and finally into the cuff of a soft wool coat—

worn by a man who did not shout,

who did not curse,

but smiled with every pitch

like he knew joy was worth remembering.


His name was Robert.

He had the shoulders of someone who carried
things for others.

The hands of a man who had learned to bless
before he learned to hold.


He had walked through city streets where people
rarely looked up—

but he looked upward often.

Even now,
as the game roared around him,
he paused...
and prayed.

Just a whisper:
"Thank You for this."

Not for victory.
Not for glory.

Just—
this.

I rested in the crease of his sleeve
as the first pitch sailed into history.
The crack of the bat,
the blur of a runner,
the eruption of the crowd—

and still,

he smiled quietly.


Not for the scoreboard.

For the moment.


Others around him screamed,

wept,

shouted with full-throated belief.


But he was still.

Watching,

soaking it in like someone

who knew the importance of letting joy be joy.


A boy beside him dropped his soda.

Robert helped him clean it up.


A woman behind him cursed the umpire.

He turned and nodded politely.

He wasn't a pope.
Not yet.

But already,
he was practicing the liturgy of kindness.

Later that night,
when the Sox won Game 1,
and Chicago danced beneath its own streetlights,
he walked home slowly—
alone,
quiet,
grinning.

The grain clung to his cuff,
then fell to the sidewalk,
carried again by wind.

But it remembered.

I have rested in the hem of prophets.

I have lingered beneath council tables.

But here—

beside a quiet man in a storm of cheers,

I saw the calm of Heaven

before the world gave him white robes.


He was a fan.

A servant.

A shepherd still in the stands.

# Chapter 15

## The Waiting

The tide whispered
like the wind once did in Galilee.

It was morning.
Gentle.
New.

The kind of morning that feels older than time.

I had been carried in a sandal,
then caught in a towel,
and now—
I lay once more
on the edge of the sea.

Not far from where it all began.

She walked slowly.
Not out of weakness,
but reverence.

Her hand rested on her belly
like a prayer made flesh.

And I,
a grain of sand touched by eternity,
felt something stir as her foot pressed into the
sand
just beside me.

She was young,
but not foolish.

Quiet,
but not alone.

There was a kind of glow in her silence—

not the kind the world captures,
but the kind Heaven watches
with breath held.

She paused,
toes curling in the warm earth,
as waves kissed her ankles
and the sun climbed the sky
with slow delight.

She looked down
and smiled.

Not at me—
at everything.

As if she heard something
no one else could hear.

A child moved within her.
She laughed softly.

Then she spoke aloud,
though no one else was near.

"You're almost here..."

Her voice cracked,
and tears slipped down,
not from sorrow,
but from knowing.

From wonder.

From the weight of waiting.

I remembered another waiting.
Another woman.
Another walk.
Another whisper in the dark
that became flesh
and changed everything.

She bent to pick up a shell.
Her hand brushed the sand.

Her fingers passed over me.

Not deeply.
Just enough to move me
slightly.

Once.

Then again.

Twice.

My breath—if I had breath—
caught in that second touch.

Not of Him...
but of something else.

Something beginning.

Something returning.

She stood.
Pressed the shell to her heart.
And continued walking.

Behind her,
the imprint of her steps
filled slowly with water,
as if the sea itself
had bowed to let her pass.

I have watched kings rise and fall.
I have rested in dust and fire,
in prisons and palaces.
I have been pressed by saints,
and carried by sinners.

But here—

in the hush of this morning,
beneath the foot of a woman
who carries more than the world can yet name—
I feel it again.

The nearness.
The breath before the Word.

He is coming.

And I remember.

# ABOUT THE AUTHOR

**JESUS J. TERAN** is a Marine Corps Veteran and life-long musician. He has been a principal of several schools in El Paso, Texas. He earned a Master of Education degree from the University of Texas at El Paso. He is married to Hortencia "Tootsie" Teran. He loves his children, grandkids, and his dog, Sadie.